W9-BZC-430

"Amazing Annabelle's class is learning about Martin Luther King Jr. Day! We follow along as Annabelle and her classmates use 21st century skills like cooperation, creativity, communication, and problem-solving as they honor his ideals and his special day.

"This book provides young readers with valuable lessons about justice and unity as they learn about the historic bus boycott with Rosa Parks during the Civil Rights Movement. The author deftly mines her own experiences as a teacher to create diverse and relatable characters that prime readers for this ongoing series."
—*Karen Littell, Principal*

"Annabelle and her schoolmates go about learning as much as they can about Martin Luther King Jr. not only during class, but also in Drama Club, during the month of January. To celebrate the accomplishments of this great man, and others who fought against segregation, like Rosa Parks, Annabelle and her friends go through an interactive classroom museum, study, write poems, and finally get to act out a special play for the whole school, and parents and friends.

"Readers who have enjoyed Annabelle in the other books in the series must read *Martin Luther King Day Jr. Day* to follow along in her discovery about an important period in the U.S."

—*Nadia Evans, Writer*

Amazing Annabelle

MARTIN LUTHER KING JR. DAY

LINDA TAYLOR
ILLUSTRATED BY KYLE HORNE

Touch Point Productions & Publishing
Long Island, NY

To my countless

students—

Oh, how you've

inspired me!

Amazing Annabelle: Martin Luther King Jr. Day
by Linda Taylor
Copyright ©2018 Linda Taylor

All rights reserved. This book is protected under the copyright laws of the United States of America. This book may not be copied or reprinted for commercial gain or profit.

ISBN 978-1-947829-04-6
For Worldwide Distribution
Printed in the U.S.A.

Touch Point Productions & Publishing Inc.
Long Island, NY
amazingannabelle.com

Contents

Martin Luther King Jr. Day Celebration

January is upon us.
Snow is on the way.
In Drama Club they're putting
   together a big production
To celebrate Dr. Martin Luther King's
   Holiday!

They're learning about his importance.
They're performing a bus
   boycott scene.
It touches many hearts and minds
As they learn about his dream.

1

HAPPY NEW YEAR!

It was New Year's Eve, and it was snowing outside! The schools were closed for the holidays, and all the students were enjoying their vacation time, especially Annabelle Copeland and her family.

Annabelle loved the holiday season, and she loved vacations even more. Her family had just returned home from their ski trip in Vermont, and now the year was about to end.

As Annabelle started writing in her special journal that she used to record memories of her unique experiences, she became a little emotional. She had created such amazing memories that she knew would last a lifetime. She had made a lot of new friends and met a lot of people who truly had a positive effect on her life this year.

This was actually her third journal because she started a new one each year. As Annabelle made her last entries for the old year, she continued to think about all the good times as well as all the bad ones. She came to the conclusion that the bad times really weren't that bad at all. They were just lessons she needed to learn for that particular time.

Annabelle thought about all the amazing things she learned, experienced, witnessed, and explored, and tried to describe every detail into her journal before the year ended. Of course she had already made some great entries, but now as she looked back at them, she needed to fine-tune the facts. She also wanted to use up the remaining pages of blank paper in her journal.

Just then, Annabelle's mom peeked into her room as she lay on her bed writing.

"Hey, Annabelle, we're starting to decorate for our New Year's party. Would you like to help us?" Mom asked.

"Sure, Mom, I'll be right down," Annabelle said with a smile.

This would be Annabelle's last celebration for the year—or would it be the first celebration for the new year? Annabelle decided it would be a little of both. She quickly wrote her last entry and then went downstairs to help decorate.

Annabelle jumped right in and started helping Alice hang some streamers in the living room. Alice began complaining and being bossy right away.

"Annabelle, you have to twist the streamers before you actually tape them up!" Alice said with an attitude.

Annabelle wondered why big sisters always have attitudes for no apparent reason. Annabelle knew about twisting the streamers and was going to do just that when she got to the other side of the room. Annabelle decided not to waste her breath by trying to explain.

Just then, Jason got ahold of the party horns and decided to use one as he ran through the house. Alice lost it and shouted at Jason.

"Can you stop with the horn already!" she yelled. "It's not time for the horn blowing! We have at least seven more hours!" Alice grabbed the horn from Jason.

Jason ran to Mom and started crying. Mom sent Alice upstairs to take a little break and let Jason go with Dad to pick up the food for their celebration so he would stop crying.

Annabelle wondered what had gotten into Alice this evening to make her act so mean. She thought, *Maybe Alice just needs an extra nap or something.*

Annabelle was fine with finishing all the decorating while Mom went upstairs to talk with Alice, although there was still a lot of decorating to do. Annabelle finished hanging the streamers from the ceiling and sprinkled silver tinsel all over the furniture and tables. She ended up blowing up seventeen balloons and taped them on the walls. She also left some on the ground to kick around. After about an hour and a half, she was finally finished. Annabelle lay on the couch to rest and eventually fell asleep.

Annabelle didn't even hear the door

open when Dad and Jason came back with all the food. When Mom came downstairs, she looked at the decorating job that Annabelle had done and was completely surprised that it looked so good. Dad was a little surprised too. Jason loved it, of course, and started kicking the balloons around the house.

When Alice came downstairs after a short nap and saw all the decorations, she started to laugh really loud. Mom and Dad started laughing as well, waking Annabelle up from her nap.

"Why is everyone laughing?" she asked, rubbing her eyes.

"We're just so happy, honey! You did an amazing job with all the decorations!" Dad said as he gave her a hug.

"Don't you think it's a little overkill?" Alice asked with a frown.

Mom replied quickly, "No, it's not. It's

just perfect, Annabelle. You did the most amazing job!"

"Great! Then let's eat because I've worked up a big appetite," Annabelle said as she got off the couch and headed toward the kitchen.

Even if the decorations were a bit much, Mom didn't care because Annabelle had done her very best to

make the house look amazing for the last celebration of the year.

The whole family sat down to eat together and shared about what had been their favorite experience the past year. Afterwards they played board games like they do every New Year's Eve. Jason couldn't keep his eyes open and eventually fell asleep on the couch during the games.

Later they turned the TV on and started watching a New Year's Eve special until it was time for the ball to drop. Everyone put their hats on and got their horns ready as the countdown started.

"10, 9, 8, 7, 6, 5, 4, 3, 2, 1, HAPPY NEW YEAR!" everyone shouted and blew their horns as loud as they could.

2

NEW YEAR'S RESOLUTIONS

Finally, it was time to go back to school again for the new year! Annabelle was excited about catching up with all her friends. There was so much lively chatter in the classroom on the first day back that Mrs. Mitchell allowed it to go on for the first ten minutes of class.

Annabelle thought Mrs. Mitchell was the absolute best teacher ever because she always did fun and interesting activities with the class. Annabelle couldn't wait to see what she had planned for the new year.

"Okay, class, our ten-minute talk time

is done. Let's settle down in our seats," Mrs. Mitchell announced.

As everyone took their seats, Mrs. Mitchell asked a very important question. "So, class, has anyone made a New Year's resolution they would like to share?"

Jake and a few other students were a little lost and weren't sure what she was talking about. He bravely raised his hand, and Mrs. Mitchell called on him.

"What is a New Year's resolution again?" Jake asked.

Annabelle spoke up before Mrs. Mitchell had a chance to answer.

"It's a decision you make to change something about yourself or do something differently in life," she said.

"Oh, then my New Year's resolution is to study more in school and get high scores on all my tests!" Jake said.

"My New Year's resolution is to try to get along with others and not always have to get my way," Victoria said, which surprised everyone.

At times Victoria could be a bit bossy and acted like she knew it all, so many of the students really liked Victoria's resolution. It came as a breath of fresh air.

Annabelle wondered what had happened to Victoria during the vacation to cause such a life-changing statement. *Was she really serious or just playing around?* Only time would tell.

"My New Year's resolution is to learn how to dance better at parties," Kaitlyn said, remembering the dancing at the Christmas celebration.

Annabelle thought Kaitlyn danced well already, but she guessed she could always learn more of the current moves.

Dexter brought up a very interesting question. "What happens if you don't fulfill your New Year's resolution halfway through the year?"

"Well," Mrs. Mitchell began, "you could always post your New Year's resolution in a special place in your house to try and remember this special promise you made. But if things go wrong and you can't get back on track, just remember, there's always next year. But always try your hardest to stick to your promise."

"My New Year's resolution is to join the Drama Club! I really want to do some new and fun things this year," Adele said with a brave smile.

Annabelle thought that was pretty bold of Adele, who was starting to come out of her shell this school year. Annabelle had just recently bonded with Adele and thought she was really nice and respectful. Now they could be in the Drama Club together!

Annabelle shared next. "My New Year's resolution is to write a book about my life here at Melville Elementary School."

One might think that Annabelle's resolution was a little unnecessary or even hard to believe, but she had already started writing her book every time she made a detailed entry into her journal.

Annabelle turned to Mrs. Mitchell and asked her what her New Year's resolution was.

"My New Year's resolution is to continue to open up a world of wonder, surprise, and learning to an awesome group of students who entered my classroom this school year," Mrs. Mitchell said, sounding like she meant it.

Annabelle thought to herself that when it comes to teachers and goals, it doesn't get any better than that.

After everyone had a chance to share their resolutions, Mrs. Mitchell announced their first big unit for the new year.

"For the month of January, we're going to recognize the accomplishments of a great leader who did so much for our country. This man spoke out against the unjust treatment African Americans were experiencing in this country many years ago. Does anyone know who I'm talking about?" Mrs. Mitchell asked.

Only a few students raised their hands to answer her question.

"Is it Dr. Martin Luther King?" Kaitlyn asked.

"Yes, it is, Kaitlyn. I noticed that not too many students raised their hand to answer that question. Once we're finished with this unit, everyone will definitely know about this great man and why we celebrate his birthday with a national holiday," Mrs. Mitchell said.

Annabelle had heard about Dr. Martin Luther King in last year's class, but she was excited about how Mrs. Mitchell would bring this unit to life and what activities she had in mind. Mrs. Mitchell made learning fun and interesting. Isabelle couldn't wait to hear more about this new unit.

3

DRAMA FOR
THE NEW YEAR

After school was the first Drama Club meeting for the new year. Annabelle wondered what Mrs. Phillips had up her sleeves for the new year. When Kaitlyn and Annabelle arrived at the auditorium, Mrs. Phillips was already there, stretching on the stage and doing warm-ups before everyone else arrived.

Annabelle thought that the class would probably do a short warm-up too before they got to their main activity. As the students slowly arrived, Mrs. Phillips instructed everyone to get on the floor

_c the warm-up exercises to take
_y any stress they might be feeling
_rom the day's activities. Annabelle really
didn't feel any stress, but she did the exercises anyway because she thought they
were a lot of fun.

Just then, Adele walked into the auditorium and looked around for someone
she knew. Adele finally made eye contact
with Annabelle, who stopped exercising
and ran down off the stage to greet her.

"Hey, Adele, I see you made it!"
Annabelle said happily.

Annabelle noticed that her friend
seemed a little nervous and shy.

"I really hope I don't regret this,"
Adele said quietly.

"Oh, of course you won't. You're going
to have the greatest time today! I guarantee it!" Annabelle declared.

Annabelle was putting her classmate's opinion of her on the line by promising a great time for Adele. But one thing Annabelle could do really well was to always have fun. She knew once the class got started, things would get interesting.

Since this was Adele's first time at Drama Club, Mrs. Phillips had everyone introduce themselves to her. Adele soon felt warm and welcome.

Then Mrs. Phillips began a quick "feelings" activity. She had a stack of cards that had a specific "feeling" word to be expressed. When a student picked a card, he or she had to silently act out that feeling in a short scene. Students could use one other student to assist them.

Jake said he would go first. After he picked a card, he chose Barry to assist him. They both acted out two brothers arguing over something. Since they had to remain silent, no one really knew exactly what they were arguing over. The audience had to figure out what feeling was being shown in the scene. Kaitlyn quickly raised her hand.

"Is the feeling anger?" she asked.

"You got it! We were arguing over who was going to pay for a pizza!" Jake shouted, happy to be successful in portraying the emotion.

The class began to laugh. Jake and Barry were really funny and did a great job.

Victoria jumped up to go next. She chose a card from the stack and then asked Kaitlyn to assist her. The two girls went off stage for a short moment to talk about it together and then came back and started acting.

Kaitlyn sat on the stage and started to fake cry. Victoria came along and began to comfort her and make her feel better. Then they walked off the stage together both smiling.

Tyler raised his hand. "Is the feeling sad?" he asked.

"Yes, but I had two feelings on my card. What was the other one?" Victoria asked.

"Happy, of course," Tyler said, sounding sure of himself.

"Correct! First, Kaitlyn was crying because she lost her dog. Then I came along and told her I would buy her a new one if we couldn't find it!"

The class clapped. They both had done a good job. It seemed as if Victoria was really trying to live up to her New Year's resolution already. She didn't cause any unnecessary drama at all. She just followed the directions and everything went well.

Annabelle chose the next card. She asked Adele to assist her, but at first she shook her head no. After the whole class encouraged her, Adele figured she could give it a try. Annabelle whispered in Adele's ear exactly what she wanted her to do. So Adele lay on the floor and pretended to be asleep. Then Annabelle ran up to her and started shaking her to wake her up. Then Annabelle pretended to tell her something with her eyes wide. They both covered their mouth with their hands and ran off the stage.

Dexter raised his hand to offer a guess. "Is the feeling scared?" he asked.

"More like terrified!" Annabelle said with excitement. "I woke Adele up to tell her that a monster was eating all our furniture and we had to get out of the house before we were next!"

The class laughed even more. The girls had done a great job, and they were definitely having fun.

After everyone had a chance to participate, Mrs. Phillips called them over to make an announcement.

"Since we celebrate Dr. Martin Luther King Jr. Day on the third Monday of January, we're going to create a short play about something important that happened in his life. When we meet tomorrow, I'll tell you about his life and introduce the play we'll perform. Happy January, and I'll see everyone tomorrow," Mrs. Phillips said with a big smile.

As all the students began to leave, there was a lot of buzz about what kind of play they would be doing and who would get the major parts. Annabelle had never been in a real play before but would definitely love the opportunity to act on a stage in front of people. She knew whatever part she was given would be fine, and she would always do her best.

Annabelle found it very interesting that Mrs. Mitchell and now Mrs. Phillips were both going to present something to their classes about Dr. Martin Luther King. Annabelle decided to do a little extra reading about him that night after she finished her homework.

4

DR. MARTIN LUTHER KING JR.

When the class came down the hall to Mrs. Mitchell's classroom the next morning, she was waiting for her students outside with the door closed. She didn't say a word and was acting very mysteriously. When all the students were finally lined up by twos, she shared with them exactly what was about to happen.

"Good morning, class. When you enter the classroom today, I want you to observe and examine everything you see. I want you to read and explore all the information you can. I also want you to listen to the sounds and voices you hear. You need to take out your notebooks and write down some notes that we'll share later. You'll have just twenty minutes to gather your information. Please go in," Mrs. Mitchell said as she opened the door.

When the students entered, they were completely shocked. Mrs. Mitchell had changed the classroom into a Dr. Martin Luther King Jr. museum! She had dozens and dozens of posters, pictures, and articles hanging on nearly every space of the walls. Mrs. Mitchell had lots of pictures and books about him on a table in the back of the room. She even had a CD of his "I Have a Dream" speech playing softly in the background.

Annabelle had never seen anything like this before in her life! Mrs. Mitchell always took her teaching and activities to the next level of excellence. Annabelle wondered how long it took Mrs. Mitchell to put this together. She thought, *Maybe she stayed in her classroom last night until ten o'clock! Or maybe she woke up this morning super early to decorate.* Whatever way she chose, she had certainly created a work of art, or should it be said a work of "heart."

The class followed Mrs. Mitchell's instructions and walked around quietly, taking in all the sights. Each student

went to as many posters and articles as they could and began to read. When they were finished, they took out their notebooks and began to write down the information they could remember.

Annabelle really wanted to capture as much as she could in words, but there just wasn't enough time. The twenty minutes was soon over, and Mrs. Mitchell told everyone to find their seats.

Mrs. Mitchell then asked the class what they learned about Dr. Martin Luther King Jr. from the notes they took during their assignment. Some students only had one or two sentences written down. Annabelle had about half a page. She wanted to write more but ran out of time.

After everyone read their brief statements, Mrs. Mitchell gave the class a short rundown about the civil rights movement. She told the students about how Dr. King and many others didn't like the bad laws that had existed in the United States many years ago.

She told them how he was a great leader and a powerful speaker who spoke out against the harmful and unjust laws against people of color. He led marches and protests, calling for fair laws for all people. Mrs. Mitchell told the class how Rosa Parks refused to give up her seat to a white man on a public bus and was arrested.

Afterwards Dr. King and many others led a protest and boycotted the public bus system, which means they refused to ride the bus. Mrs. Mitchell also explained how Dr. King led peaceful protests and fought the unjust laws without rough physical force. Dr. King once said they should drive out hatred in America with love.

The whole class listened closely to each word that came out of Mrs. Mitchell's mouth. After she spoke, she showed her students a short non-fiction video about the life of Dr. King. After the video, the class was in a serious mood.

"How could people treat others like that? I think it's just plain wrong," Barry said angrily.

"You got that right," agreed Jake. "If I was there, I would definitely have helped Dr. King and marched with him."

"Dr. King and all those other protesters were so brave. I mean, they were attacked by dogs and water hoses!" Kaitlyn said, her voice rising higher.

"My dad is a firefighter," added Tyler, "and I've seen water come out of those hoses. It's really strong and can knock a person down."

"But just think about it, if those brave

men and women didn't fight for equal rights, our country would probably be a different kind of place right now," Annabelle said.

"My dad says we should always fight for what we know is right," Adele added.

"We should never let people take advantage of others or treat anyone in a way that's not fair," Dexter said.

Mrs. Mitchell knew the video would spark a good discussion, and she was really pleased by all the comments and class participation.

"It seems as if everyone really learned some important information from our classroom museum and the video. Now, here is your task. Every group needs to come up with a skit, poem, song, or story that honors the life and ideals of Dr. Martin Luther King. I'm going to give everyone a list of words to consider using for your activity. And this time, you will be able to pick your own groups just as long as everyone is included," Mrs. Mitchell said.

This was the very first time Mrs. Mitchell allowed the class to pick their own partners. As everyone came together to form their groups, Mrs. Mitchell made sure that everything went smoothly and that everyone was included and felt comfortable in their group.

Annabelle was in a group with Kaitlyn, Adele, and Victoria. Annabelle had never been in an all-girl group before. Since they were all friends, she thought it would go well. Annabelle would have to find out tomorrow since class was now over.

5

DRAMA PLAY

Annabelle felt full of knowledge about Dr. King as she left Mrs. Mitchell's class. She couldn't wait to start working with her group on the project. But right then, it was Drama Club time. Annabelle remembered that Mrs. Phillips said she was going to introduce a play involving Dr. King today, and she was really excited about it.

When all the students entered the auditorium, they noticed a lot of chairs sitting on the stage. They were arranged in two straight rows facing the side of the stage with one single chair in the front.

Everyone wondered what was going to happen. Finally, Mrs. Phillips came into the auditorium and gathered all the students together.

"Welcome, my fellow thespians! As you can see, the stage is set for our first rehearsal of our Dr. Martin Luther King play!" Mrs. Phillips announced.

The students were a little confused by being called thespians. Apparently, no one knew what a thespian was. Jake raised his hand to ask.

"Mrs. Phillips, what on earth is a thespian? I don't know if I really like the sound of that word right now," he admitted.

Mrs. Phillips laughed before giving her answer. "A thespian is just a fancy way of saying actor or actress in the theater world," she explained. "I think very highly of each one of you. All of you have superb acting skills, which is why I know everyone will do a tremendous job with this play!"

"Exactly what is it about anyway?" asked Victoria. "You never told us the plot."

"All in good time, Victoria. I want you to feel this play as I explain its contents to you. The two rows of chairs you see in front of you represent the seats on a bus. I want Barry to come up and sit in this front chair and be the bus driver. Jake and Tyler, I want you to stand on the side and be the police officers. Annabelle, I want you to be a seamstress named Rosa Parks. I'll tell you when to enter the bus. Everyone else, I need you to fill the seats on the bus. Now let's get into our places everyone," Mrs. Phillips directed.

Everyone moved into place just as their teacher had told them. Then Mrs.

Phillips began telling the true story of Rosa Parks.

"One day in Montgomery, Alabama, a seamstress, which is a woman who sews for a living, named Rosa Parks had just put in a long hard day at work and was boarding a bus to go home. She paid her fare in the front of the bus, got out, and then re-entered through the side entrance and sat in the back in what they called the 'colored' section," Mrs. Phillips explained, speaking with a southern sounding voice.

Mrs. Phillips paused to give direction to Annabelle, who was playing the part of Rosa. Mrs. Phillips told the students that this story took place in 1955 when all public buses were segregated. At that time in history, segregation was written into law, even though it was very wrong and unfair. The white passengers sat in the front of the bus in the "white" section, and black passengers had to sit in the back of the bus in the "colored" section.

Mrs. Phillips continued telling the story. "While on route, they came to a bus stop. A white man climbed into the bus. Finding no seat in the white section, he went up to the bus driver and demanded that he find him a seat. So the driver told all the black passengers in the first row of the colored section to stand and move to the back so the white man could sit in that row. This added another row to the white section. Three of the four black passengers on that row moved, but Rosa Parks did not."

Mrs. Phillips paused again to give direction to the students playing the parts of the bus driver, the white passenger, and Rosa.

"The driver told Rosa to get out of her

seat, but she wouldn't move," continued Mrs. Phillips. "She was tired of her people always giving in, when she knew this law was unfair to black people. In a short while, two police officers came into the bus and arrested Rosa Parks."

Mrs. Phillips gave the appropriate directions to the characters playing specific roles. After the police officers took Rosa off stage, the white man sat down. At that point, Mrs. Phillips asked all the bus passengers to quietly lift their chairs up and take them off stage. As they were doing that, Mrs. Phillips started singing an old Negro spiritual called, "I've Been 'Buked."

With curious looks on their faces, the students watched and listened to Mrs. Phillips sing. After she finished the first two verses of the song, she explained the lyrics to the class and why she chose that selection. She told the students that the word *'buked* from the song was short for the word rebuked, which means to express sharp disapproval and criticism of someone.

She told them how some white people treated black people this way for many years. She also explained the word *scorn* in the song, which means a strong feeling of no respect for someone. The scene they just acted out clearly showed those two words that were used in the song.

Mrs. Phillips told them that she needed a special song to be sung after that scene so the actors could clear away the chairs and prepare for the next scene.

The next scene involved a boycott of riding on public buses. This boycott was led by none other than Dr. Martin Luther King Jr. himself. He was just a twenty-six-year-old preacher at the time, but he was a powerful speaker who declared the truth to the leaders at that particular time in history.

For the boycott scene, Mrs. Phillips had made many large protest signs for the students to carry. After reading some explanation that set the stage for the next scene, Mrs. Phillips instructed the students to hold up the signs and walk

around in a circle. Once a line across the stage was formed, each student in turn yelled out the words on their sign to the audience. After the last person spoke, everyone yelled out, "EQUAL RIGHTS FOR ALL!" five times and walked off the stage.

The students really got into that scene. They felt a sense of teamwork and unity, fighting for the same ideals as Dr. King and so many others had done during that time, which is known as the civil rights movement.

The last scene in the play highlighted Dr. Martin Luther King's most famous speech, "I Have a Dream." She chose Jamal to be Dr. Martin Luther King, and he read a portion of the speech very well. The class cheered afterwards and sang the song, "This Little Light of Mine." After some closing narration, the play was complete. Everyone loved it!

6

REHEARSAL AFTERMATH

Annabelle was on cloud nine with all her newfound Dr. Martin Luther King Jr. knowledge! All the students from the Drama Club couldn't stop talking about the play they had just acted out with Mrs. Phillips. The bus ride home was lively with many comments and questions shared.

"That was a really good play Mrs. Phillips put together today. I wonder when we're going to actually perform it," Kaitlyn said.

"Probably for some assembly at school," Jake said.

Adele became a little nervous. "You mean for the whole entire school! We're really going to perform this play on the stage for the whole school?"

"Sure, what's wrong with that?" asked Annabelle. "There's really nothing to be nervous about. You did a great job, Adele, even if it's just your second day of Drama Club. You're a natural!" Annabelle said, trying to calm and encourage her friend.

"There's always some kind of assembly for Dr. King's holiday," said Barry. "Remember last year we had that motivational speaker come in who had us yelling out some positive phrases from the audience? He was really good. I remember the chorus sang a few songs too."

"But only two weeks are left before Dr. King's holiday." Adele groaned. "We don't even have enough time to get everything together!"

"Oh ye of little faith. We have plenty of time, Adele," Annabelle said to encourage her friend. "Our very first rehearsal today was awesome! All we have to do now is learn a few lines and we're set. I feel very confident that we'll definitely be ready."

Victoria spoke up. "I agree with Annabelle. There's not much to say or memorize for this play. It's pretty simple and straightforward. I think I'd like to be the one to read some of the narration. The reading really moves the play along nicely."

Once again, Annabelle was surprised by Victoria's positive comments. Her resolution promises were being utilized yet again. Annabelle could definitely get used to this. She was beginning to look at Victoria in a different light. Annabelle hoped this was a sign of good things to come, especially since they were in the same group for the Dr. King project in Mrs. Mitchell's class.

Some of the students began to think about what they would personally do if they had lived during the civil rights movement.

Dexter began to take a bold attitude as he spoke from his seat. "Man, if I was alive during the time of Rosa Parks, I would've stayed in my seat too if some white bus driver asked me to give up my seat to a white man."

"Me too! I probably would have told the white man to stand up or just wait for another bus," Tyler agreed.

Jamal, who had been pretty quiet until now, finally spoke up from his seat in the middle of the bus. "Both of you need to understand what was really going on during those times. Remember, Mrs. Phillips said that segregation was the law of the land. During that time, if you didn't obey the law, you were going to jail."

"That's right, and Rosa Parks was really a brave woman to do what she did," Annabelle added. "I mean, she lost her job and was harassed by a lot of people for standing up for justice. It's a good thing she had Dr. King and strong support systems behind her like the NAACP."

"What is the NAACP?" Tyler asked, frowning at the strange initials.

"NAACP stands for the National Association for the Advancement of Colored People. Both Rosa and her husband were members of this group as were many other people of color around the country," Annabelle explained.

Annabelle felt good that she had done her research on Dr. King and the civil rights movement when Mrs. Mitchell first introduced it in class. Annabelle was also impressed to hear Jamal open up and make a comment on the bus. He was usually quiet and reserved.

Jamal's dad was the preacher down at First Baptist Church where Annabelle's family attended every Sunday. He always sat on the first row with his whole family to hear his dad preach. Annabelle thought very highly of Jamal and thought he was a good choice to play the part of Dr. King in the play.

"Annabelle, why is it that you always know so much about everything?" Victoria asked what other students sometimes wondered.

"Oh, I don't know everything, but I just like to study about special topics. When Mrs. Mitchell mentioned Dr. King, I just thought it was a good idea to learn more about him on my own. It's really no big deal," Annabelle said humbly.

"Actually, my dad says it is a big deal to know about your history and things that have happened in this world. I think Annabelle just likes to stay ahead of the game," Jamal said.

Well, Annabelle certainly wasn't going to argue with that reasoning because she knew it was true. Annabelle was glad to hear Jamal speak up once again and make some positive remarks about her. Annabelle was really starting to like Jamal more and more, as a friend of course. She couldn't wait to see his performance as Dr. King in the play.

7

SNOW DAY

The next morning, Annabelle was excited about going to school and starting the Dr. King assignment. Unfortunately, everything would have to be put on hold due to the heavy snowstorm that had started during the night and continued all day long.

Annabelle hadn't seen this coming. But then again, she hadn't listened to the weather report the night before. All the schools in her district were closed, and even her mom and dad stayed home from work. It was an outright snow day, and Annabelle and her brother Jason wanted to take advantage of this day off from school.

First of all, they were able to spend more time in their comfy beds. After the alarm clock woke her up and her mom told her it was a snow day, Annabelle went back to sleep for three hours! She hadn't realized how much sleep she needed to catch up on. The rest of her family had gone back to bed too. Getting some extra sleep is always a wonderful thing.

When Annabelle finally woke up for the second time, she slowly rolled out of bed and went downstairs. Her mom was fixing a big breakfast just as she did on Sunday mornings.

Annabelle always buttered the biscuits and poured the juice. Alice was already downstairs setting the table. When breakfast was ready, the whole family came to the table and ate together, which was very rare for a weekday. Annabelle thought this was such a special time because she unexpectedly had a free day to share bonding time with her family.

"Mom, everything is so delicious as usual. I really love the buttermilk biscuits," Annabelle said before she took her last bite.

"Well, thank you, honey. So what plans do you have today?"

"Since everyone is home today," Annabelle said, "I thought maybe we could take advantage of some family time and play a game of Pictionary together." Annabelle began to get excited.

"I love Pictionary!" said Jason. "Yeah, let's do that, Mom!"

"Oh, will you look at the time?" said Alice quickly. "I definitely have to call two of my friends and then catch up on some reading. Maybe I'll join you some other time," she said as she started to get up from the table.

"I'm all in!" said Dad. "I just have to make a conference call at one o'clock and then I'm free."

"I'm available all day long so I'm in too," said Mom. "Alice, why don't you make your calls after you clean up the kitchen, and we can all play at about three o'clock? I'm sure you can take a break from your reading for a short while to spend some quality time with your family, right?" Mom suggested.

"It all depends on how long it takes me to do all these dishes," Alice said.

"I'll help you, Alice," offered Annabelle. "I'll clean off the table and put everything away, and you can just put the dirty dishes in the dishwasher. We'll be finished in no time."

"I guess that could work," said Alice. "I do have some other projects I have to do too, but I'll make some time in my day to play Pictionary with you."

"That's great!" cried Annabelle. "We'll all meet back here at the dining room table at three o'clock sharp."

Everyone agreed. After Annabelle helped Alice with the dishes, she went to her room to do a little planning for her upcoming project. Annabelle made a list of some possible ideas they could do in their group that would show the ideals of Dr. King.

She didn't want anyone in the group to think she was trying to take over or be in charge, but it was just Annabelle's nature to plan ahead and make suggestions. She couldn't help herself. Sometimes Annabelle thought she had an automatic thinking switch that turned on early in the morning and only went off at night.

Right at that moment, a lightbulb turned on in Annabelle's mind. She had a great idea for a poem she wanted to write. She immediately sat at her desk with her rhyming dictionary and went to work. As time passed, she realized she had written an awesome Dr. King poem that went like this:

Dr. Martin Luther King Jr.

Dr. Martin Luther King
    was a great man.
He gave many speeches
    around many lands.
He spoke of freedom.
He spoke of truth.
He spoke to the old.
He spoke to the youth.
He spoke of peace and unity,
So the world could be a better place
    for you and me.

Dr. King was great. Dr. King was grand.
Dr. King was the man:
The man to make a stand!
For the rights of our people
    who've been held down.
To make a stand!
For our people who've
    been pushed around.
To make a stand!
So black and white can live in unity.
So the world could be
A better place for you and me.

Dr. King was brave.
Dr. King was strong.
There were some that thought
    he was wrong.
He kept his faith. He kept his dream.
Dr. King was on the winning team.

We remember him in a special way.
Now he has a holiday!

Dr. King fought nonviolently.
So the world could be
A better place for you and me.

After she finished this poem, she felt energized! She couldn't believe she wrote such a long poem on a snow day! Annabelle felt very good about it and couldn't wait to share it with Mrs. Mitchell. She didn't want it to be part of her group assignment but thought maybe it could be recited during the Dr. King program at school. After her thoughts started to wind down about school stuff, she decided she needed a change of pace.

Annabelle got dressed in her coat, winter boots, hat, scarf, and gloves and went outside to play in the snow with Jason. They built a snowman together and made snow angels. Dad came out later and shoveled the driveway and sidewalks while Annabelle and Jason helped clean the snow off his car. When they were finished, they threw a few snowballs at each other for fun. When they became really cold, they went back inside. They tracked so much snow into the house that Mom had to bring some towels to the front door to dry the floor off.

Mom prepared some hot cocoa with big marshmallows and whipped cream for the entire family. After Annabelle, Jason, and Dad got warm again, they noticed that it was three o'clock and time for Pictionary. They all gathered around the table and brought out the big easel with chart paper so they could each draw their pictures for the game. Then the fun and laughter began.

After the game, Dad drove in the snow to get pizza for dinner and ice cream for dessert. Mom made a healthy salad to go with the pizza. After their meal, Dad opened a joke book and told corny jokes for the rest of the night. This was the first fun snow day for the school year. Annabelle loved days like this when nothing else really mattered except family and fun.

8

DR. KING ASSIGNMENT

Once again, Annabelle woke up excited about going to school and starting her Dr. King assignment. She looked outside, and everything looked like a winter wonderland because a lot of snow was still on the ground from yesterday.

All the schools had a two-hour delayed opening, giving the snow plows time to finish clearing the streets. This time, Annabelle went back to sleep for one hour and then had to wake up and get ready for school. She knew it was going to be a short day and hoped it would go by quickly so they could go to Drama Club.

When the students arrived at school, they all shared their snowy day stories and adventures. Then Mrs. Mitchell got right down to the business of their Dr. King assignments.

First, she let the students listen to Dr. King's famous "I Have a Dream" speech. She hoped it would stir the students' interest and creativity as they heard his powerful words.

Then Mrs. Mitchell gave a quick review of what the students were supposed to do and what was expected from each group. She had them use the remaining time in the period to break into groups and get started.

Annabelle saw this as the perfect time to share her poem with Mrs. Mitchell. She went over to the teacher's desk and began telling her about the poem and handed it to her to read. As Mrs. Mitchell read the poem, she had a happy look on her face and told Annabelle how much she loved it. Mrs. Mitchell thought it was a wonderful idea to present this poem at the Dr. King assembly.

Since Annabelle already had a key role in the Dr. King play, Mrs. Mitchell suggested the poem be broken up into three sections, allowing three other students to recite it. Annabelle liked the idea and was very excited that the whole school would get to hear it.

Annabelle, Kaitlyn, Adele, and Victoria assembled in the back corner of the room and started brainstorming ideas for their project. Annabelle took her notebook out with ideas and suggestions she had already come up with yesterday. Each group had a copy of the list of words Mrs. Mitchell gave them to spark their interest.

Victoria began, "I like the word *justice* because Dr. King fought for justice for all people."

"That's a good idea," Annabelle said, supporting her friend. "Maybe we can use that word in a poem about him."

Annabelle was trying to be as low-key as possible, trying not to act as if she were in charge. She wanted to see what ideas everyone else would come up with before introducing hers. Annabelle would support any idea that sounded good, and she really wanted to give everyone else a chance.

"Do you think we could do an acrostic poem for the word justice," asked Adele, "where the first line starts with the letter J, the second line starts with the letter U, and so on until the word is spelled out? Or we could just write a different kind of poem."

"I guess we could do it either way," said Annabelle. "We just have to decide which one."

"I think we should do a poem both ways and see which one is better," Kaitlyn suggested.

"Okay, what do you say if we try the acrostic poem first and see what we come up with?" Annabelle asked the group.

Seeing everyone nod their heads in agreement, Victoria asked, "Who's going to be the recorder? I have horrible handwriting."

Annabelle quickly offered to do it and turned to a clean page in her notebook.

"Okay, let's think of a catchy phrase for the letter J," said Annabelle. "How about this: J is for joyful, that's how the people felt when Dr. King gave his speeches. His presence was heartfelt."

"Hey, that's pretty cool Annabelle!" said Adele. "You really have a talent for writing poetry."

"I have this rhyming dictionary if anyone wants to use it," Annabelle offered. "It helps me find rhymes to just about any word."

Everyone started looking in the rhyming dictionary and finding some words they wanted to use. After a short while, Kaitlyn tried her hand at a catchy phrase.

"Okay," she said, "I think I have a line for U. Listen to this: U is for understanding, Dr. King really was. When he came onto the scene, so fresh and clean, his presence caused a buzz."

"Kaitlyn, that's an awesome rhyme! You really nailed it, girl! I like that one a lot!" Annabelle said as she gave her a high five.

Victoria spoke up excitedly, "Okay, okay, check this out. I got the next line. S is for serious. Dr. King was a serious man. He gave speeches all around. He had a really great plan."

"Wow, I can't believe we already have all these great lines! We're doing a great job!" Annabelle exclaimed.

"Okay, here's my line," said Adele. "T is for trust. He had the people's trust. If you want to lead anyone, this really is a must."

It seemed as if the rhyming dictionary was helping everyone in their group come up with catchy phrases in the poem. Annabelle was happy that she brought it to school because it was definitely a great tool.

"I is for important," said Annabelle. "Dr. King did important things. He helped to change a lot of terrible laws and helped make freedom ring."

Kaitlyn spoke up next. "C is for courage. It took courage to fight the good fight. He wanted all people to unite together. It shouldn't matter if you're black or white."

"E is for excellent," added Victoria to finish off the poem. "Dr. King made a difference in this world. He was a man of excellence. He helped every man, woman, boy, and girl."

And on that note, the bell rang, and they were finished with their project. Annabelle couldn't believe how quickly the time went and how great their group worked together. Annabelle felt confident that the poem they just created honored the life and ideals of Dr. King.

This is the poem in its entirety:

J-U-S-T-I-C-E

J is for JOYFUL, that's how the people felt when Dr. King gave his speeches. His presence was heartfelt.

U is for UNDERSTANDING. Dr. King really was. When he came onto the scene, so fresh and clean, his presence caused a buzz.

S is for SERIOUS. Dr. King was a

serious man. He gave speeches all around. He had a really great plan.

T is for TRUST. He had the people's trust. If you want to lead anyone, this really is a must.

I is for IMPORTANT. Dr. King did important things. He helped to change a lot of terrible laws and helped make freedom ring.

C is for COURAGE. It took courage to fight the good fight. He wanted all people to unite together. It shouldn't matter if you're black or white.

E is for EXCELLENT. Dr. King made a difference in this world. He was a man of excellence. He helped every man, woman, boy, and girl.

9

CHURCH DAY

During one of the last practices for the Drama Club play, everyone was really getting into their parts. Each one had their lines memorized and knew where to stand and which props to use. The backstage crew got their act together as well. Everything was really coming together.

One of the best highlights of the play was the Dr. King speech given by Jamal. He really put a lot of work into making his voice sound older and stronger. Jamal's voice reminded Annabelle of Jamal's father, the Reverend Wendell Davis at Faith Baptist Church. When Jamal delivered the Dr. King speech, the whole auditorium became super silent. Everyone listened intently to Dr. King's moving words spoken by Jamal with style and grace.

Annabelle knew that when Jamal delivered that speech on the day of the performance, it would definitely bring the house down for sure. Little did Jamal know, he would actually get the opportunity to deliver the speech even earlier to a different audience.

When Sunday rolled around, the entire Copeland family attended Faith Baptist Church as they did every Sunday. However, this Sunday the congregation would be in for a big surprise.

Annabelle and Alice sang in the youth choir along with Jamal, his older brother, Jared, and his younger sister, Janiyah. The choir sang two upbeat songs that were well-received by loud clapping from the congregation.

Annabelle's mom always told her that the older members loved to encourage the young people because they knew that the young people could be doing a lot of other things rather than being so active in church activities. She also said that it was so important to let young people know that they're needed and appreciated. As a result, most likely they would grow up to be well-rounded individuals in society.

After the youth choir sang, Jamal and Jared didn't go right back to the choir stand where the other choir members sat. They mysteriously went to the back of the church. Reverend Davis stood up at the podium in the pulpit and praised the youth for their participation in the service as he had earlier praised the liturgical dancers for their dance selection.

Annabelle thought Reverend Davis was a fun pastor who loved to build up the youth and encourage them any chance he could. He once played a game of kickball with all the young people during the church picnic at Tanner Park during summer vacation.

Reverend Davis began talking about Dr. Martin Luther King's holiday that was coming up the next week. He spoke about the importance of celebrating this special holiday because of all Dr. King had done to make this country a better place for all of them to live.

Reverend Davis also knew about the Dr. Martin Luther King play at Melville School that Friday. He started talking about it and how some of the youth from Faith Baptist Church had major roles. Reverend Davis announced Annabelle's name as the actress playing the part of Rosa Parks and asked her to stand up to be recognized. Once again, the congregation clapped loudly.

Annabelle felt like a real star in her own church! But she wouldn't let this attention go to her head. Her mom always told her to take things in stride and be humble when others praised her. Annabelle slowly stood up for a second, waved her hand to the congregation, then quickly sat back down.

Then Reverend Davis shared that his son Jamal would be the actor playing the role of Dr. Martin Luther King in the play. Just as this was announced, Jared, Jamal's older brother, and his friend Bailey walked down the middle aisle with dark shades on, pretending to be secret service agents. Jamal wore a black robe and followed closely behind them, acting out the role of Dr. Martin Luther King.

Jamal walked slowly and confidently

to the podium and delivered a large portion of Dr. King's famous speech, "I Have a Dream." His voice was crisp and clear and rang out powerfully to the congregation.

After he spoke the last words, "Free at last, free at last, thank God Almighty, we are free at last," the entire congregation were on their feet clapping so loud it

sounded like a thunderstorm, for what seemed like a full five minutes!

Reverend Davis shook his hand and then gave him a big hug. The audience continued clapping. Annabelle had never seen such a wonderful and moving performance in her life. Her eyes filling up with tears of joy as she watched Reverend Davis hug Jamal.

Reverend Davis praised his son for a wonderful portrayal of Dr. Martin Luther King. Thinking about it, Annabelle realized that the speech was really a lot to memorize! Annabelle was so proud of Jamal because he had truly nailed it. She was excitedly looking forward to the full performance of the play on Friday at Melville School.

10

DR. KING PERFORMANCE

Annabelle couldn't wait to get to school the next day and share with Mrs. Phillips and the whole Drama Club what took place on Sunday at church. However, Annabelle wasn't the only one sharing that particular information. Other students from her school who also attended Faith Baptist Church were talking about the performance too.

Jamal was definitely the most talked about student on Monday. It's as if he had just become very popular overnight. Students who would normally not give him the time of day were suddenly talking with him for a long time. Jamal was the center of attention for most of the morning.

But after a while, his accomplishment became old news and the excitement died down. Jamal was sort of glad about that because he was low-key and modest. He was just happy that he was able to play the role of such an important man whom he truly admired as a great leader of our country. Jamal wasn't a bragger and didn't like when all the attention was on him. It was Jamal's hope that students would channel that energy into learning more about the real Dr. King.

Annabelle thought that Jamal was very much like Dr. King because his dad was a preacher, just like Dr. King's dad was a preacher. She also thought that maybe Jamal would grow up and be a preacher one day, just like his own dad had done. Annabelle wondered how Jamal felt about these similarities, so she boldly asked him during indoor recess.

"Hey, Jamal, I have a question for you. Do you think you'll be a preacher like your dad and Dr. King when you grow up?"

"I know my dad would love it if I did become a preacher," said Jamal. "He's always telling me and many, many others that I'm going to be a preacher one day when I grow up. Honestly, I just don't know right now."

"That's a fair answer," said Annabelle. "I mean, you're just a kid right now. Who really knows what the future holds? Just for the record, I think you'd make a really cool preacher, just like your dad. You have a really great speaking voice."

"Thanks, Annabelle. I'll remember that," Jamal said with a big smile.

A new and promising friendship was

forged at that very moment. Annabelle really valued her friends and noticed that she and Jamal shared a common bond—their involvement in church. Annabelle was pretty happy about that.

When Friday finally arrived, the whole school was buzzing about the Dr. Martin Luther King Jr. Day assembly. Mrs. Phillips arranged for all the Drama Club students to come down to the auditorium first thing in the morning. They set up the stage, got dressed in costumes, found their props, and were ready for the first performance. They would give a second performance that evening for the school administration, parents, friends, and anyone who wanted to see the performance again.

Mrs. Phillips gave everyone a pep talk before the performance. She warned the students that if anything went wrong, they shouldn't stop because the show must go on. She said to never let the audience know if a mistake was made. Mrs. Phillips also reminded the students that if anything went wrong, they must improvise, improvise, improvise. Annabelle remembered that the Drama Club had a lot of practice with improvisational games during their regular sessions.

All the classes in the whole building were entering the auditorium one by one and filing into the seats. First the kindergarteners followed by the first-, second-, third-, fourth-, and fifth-graders. When all the classes were seated, the principal, Mr. Jefferson, walked to the microphone and had everyone stand for the Pledge of Allegiance and the song, "My Country 'Tis of Thee."

Afterwards he instructed everyone to look at the big projector screen that had the words to the Black National Anthem, "Lift Ev'ry Voice and Sing." Everyone sang this song nicely and loudly, following the words on the screen.

Mr. Jefferson gave a little welcome address and talked about the purpose of the assembly. He gave a brief statement about Dr. Martin Luther King Jr. Day and how it all started. He didn't want to take up too much time because there was so much on the program.

He introduced Mrs. Phillips, who gave a short introduction of the play the audience was about to see. She didn't speak long at all because her students had narration parts that were going to move the play along.

Finally, the curtain opened and the students acted out the bus scene. They did it perfectly just as they had practiced many times before. No one seemed to be nervous as they confidently said their lines. Annabelle held a wireless microphone as she sat on the bus and spoke clearly while saying her famous Rosa Parks' lines.

After scene one, Mrs. Phillips had arranged for the chorus to sing the Negro spiritual, "I've Been 'Buked" while they set up for scene two behind the curtains.

When the curtain opened for scene two, all the students had their protest

signs and marched around in a circle. Each protestor yelled out the words on their individual sign perfectly. After they marched off the stage saying the "Equal Rights for All" chant, the curtains closed. The chorus came onto the stage again to sing two more songs.

When the curtains opened for scene three, some students were cheering as two secret service men brought Dr. Martin Luther King Jr., played by none other than Jamal Davis, up to the stage. Once again, he did a magnificent job and the audience stood and clapped for him at the end. The chorus came onto the stage again and sang the final two songs with the Drama Club members. The first official performance was over.

Mrs. Mitchell walked to the podium and announced another presentation of a special poem that was written by one of the students at Melville School. It was the Dr. King poem Annabelle had written. Mrs. Mitchell had practiced with three students in a fifth-grade class after school to recite this poem in a special way. Annabelle was so excited about the play that she had completely forgotten about the poem. Mrs. Mitchell had surprised her as well as the class.

The three students recited the poem in a rap form. As the audience listened to the three boys, the audience began to clap with the beat of their voices. The audience loved the poem and clapped loudly. Annabelle stood beaming with pride.

Mr. Jefferson gave a few closing remarks and the assembly was over. He instructed all the teachers to talk about Dr. Martin Luther King with their students when they got back to their classrooms.

Annabelle was hopeful that this performance really affected the students in a positive way. She couldn't wait to do the whole performance again in the evening for her parents.

When the drama students in Mrs. Mitchell's class returned to the classroom, all the other students cheered. Mrs. Mitchell was so proud of everyone. Annabelle thanked Mrs. Mitchell for remembering her poem and having it presented in that way. It brought joy to her heart.

Mrs. Mitchell gave everyone a Dr. King packet with lots of fun learning activities to complete in class. This Dr. King Celebration Day made it a fun Friday for the entire school.

Annabelle thought to herself, *What a great way to end the week!* She hoped everyone would remember Dr. Martin Luther King's holiday each and every year.

ANNABELLE'S DISCUSSION CORNER

1. Why does this country celebrate Dr. Martin Luther King with a national holiday?

2. If you were in a Dr. King play in a Drama Club, what part would you like to have and why?

3. List three or four things you would do on a snowy day.

Don't miss Annabelle's other amazing books!

Amazing Annabelle and the Apple Celebration

Amazing Annabelle and the Fall Festival

Amazing Annabelle—Thank You, Veterans!

Amazing Annabelle and December Celebrations

ABOUT THE AUTHOR

 Linda Taylor has been teaching students for over 25 years. She enjoys connecting with students on many levels. She also loves writing poetry. Linda lives on Long Island, New York.

ABOUT THE ILLUSTRATOR

 Kyle Horne has a B.A. in Visual Communications from S.U.N.Y. Old Westbury College in New York. Kyle has displayed his artwork in many local libraries. He lives on Long Island.